POKÉMON

Pikachu in Love

Adapted by
Tracey West

OFFICIAL
POKÉMON
EXPERT'S
CLUB

SCHOLASTIC INC.
New York Toronto London Auckland Sydney
Mexico City New Delhi Hong Kong Buenos Aires

Published by Scholastic Inc.
90 Old Sherman Turnpike, Danbury, CT 06816.

SCHOLASTIC and associated logos are trademarks and/or registered trademarks of Scholastic Inc.

ISBN-10: 0-439-72187-3
ISBN-13: 978-0-439-72187-5

First Scholastic Printing, April 2005

Ash and his friends always meet strange Pokémon on their adventures.

But one day, they met a strange *person*. Pikachu was surprised.

"I am Old Man Shuckle," said the little man. "I make special medicine for Pokémon."

"*Pika?*" asked Pikachu.

"How do you do that?" Brock asked.

"It is a secret," said Old Man Shuckle. "I use a Pokémon called Shuckle."

"Please tell me!" Brock begged.

Old Man Shuckle explained each step.

First he put secret ingredients inside the Shuckle shell.

Then he let the Shuckle loose in the wild.

A year later, he found the Shuckle
again. Then he took the juice out
of the shell.

"There is even a special kind of juice that can make any Pokémon easy to catch and train," said the old man. "To make it, you must use a rare blue Shuckle."

"Easy-to-train Pokémon!" Brock said. "If I had that juice, I could become the world's best Pokémon Trainer."

"I can give you some of that juice," said Old Man Shuckle. "But you and your friends must help me."

Old Man Shuckle called for his Bellsprout. "This is Spoopie," he said. "Spoopie can sniff out wild Shuckle. I need you to follow Spoopie and collect the blue Shuckle for me," said Old Man Shuckle.

"We will help!" said Brock. Ash and Misty agreed.

"*Pika!*" said Pikachu.

"*Togi, togi,*" said Togepi.

The friends followed Spoopie into the woods.

Spoopie sniffed the air. Then it began to run.

"That Spoopie is very speedy!" said Misty.

The friends chased Spoopie
through the woods.

Spoopie found lots of Shuckle. It threw the Shuckle into the air for the others to catch.

"It is like a Shuckle shower!" Ash cried.

Then Spoopie ran off again.

"Slow down, Spoopie!" Brock called out.

Spoopie sniffed and sniffed. It finally found the rare blue Shuckle!

Suddenly Team Rocket dropped down from the trees.

"The blue Shuckle is ours now!" Jessie cried.

"Weezing, use Smokescreen!"
James yelled.
Thick smoke filled the air.
Team Rocket grabbed the blue
Shuckle and ran and ran.

"I am thirsty!" Jessie said.
Team Rocket did not have water.
They drank the juice from the blue
Shuckle!

Meowth started to feel a little strange. "I love you, James!" Meowth said. Then it gave James a big hug and a kiss.

Nearby, the wild Shuckle began to move.

"Where are they going?" asked Ash.

"Someone drank the blue Shuckle juice," Old Man Shuckle said. "You should not drink it right from the shell. If you do, it makes Pokémon fall in love with you!"

The Shuckle were all in love
with Jessie. They licked her face.
"Yuck!" Jessie yelled.
She ran away.

Team Rocket ran right into Ash and his friends.

"Give that blue Shuckle back right now!" Misty said.

"We will fight you first!" Jessie said. She called on Wobbuffet and Arbok.

But the Pokémon did not want to fight. They wanted to hug Jessie instead!

"Great!" Ash said. "Pikachu,
use Thunderbolt!"

But Pikachu did not attack.
It was in love with Jessie, too!

Old Man Shuckle ran up.
"This has gone too far!" he said.
Then he sprinkled a powder on all
of the Pokémon.

"The powder has cured the Pokémon," said Old Man Shuckle. He was right. The Pokémon were not in love with Jessie and James anymore.

Spoopie made the first move.
It used Vine Whip to take the blue
Shuckle from Jessie's arms.

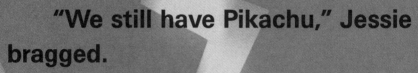

"We still have Pikachu," Jessie bragged.

But Pikachu was not in love with Jessie anymore, either.

"Pikachuuuuuuu!" Pikachu shocke Team Rocket. They went blasting off again.

"Thank you for finding the blue Shuckle, Brock," Old Man Shuckle said. "Here is the special juice I promised you. You can use it to catch and train any Pokémon."

"No thanks," Brock said. "I want Pokémon to love me for who I am—not because of any juice."

"I think they already do," said Ash.

"Pika!" Pikachu agreed.

Who's That Rock Pokémon?

See page 45 or your
Rock & Ground Pokédex
for the answer.

A Rock/Ground Challenge

One of the Pokémon in each row is a Rock Type. The other is a Ground Type. Can you tell which Pokémon is which Type?

1. Cubone™   Sudowoodo™

2. Gligar™   Aerodactyl™

3. Lunatone™   Baltoy™

4. Steelix™   Aron™

5. Relicanth™   Wooper™

6. Nosepass™   Donphan™

7. Anorith™   Diglett™

39

Check page 45 or your *Rock & Ground Pokédex* for the answers.

Battle Time!

Now it is your turn to battle! Read about each battle below. Then pick the best Pokémon to use against your opponent. In each battle, all of the Pokémon are the same level.

1. *Bam! Bam!* Here comes Regirock, a tough Rock Pokémon. Which of these Pokémon will last the longest in battle?

| Quilava™ | Glalie™ | Makuhita™ |
| (Fire) | (Ice) | (Fighting) |

2. Your opponent throws out Sandslash, a Ground Pokémon. Which Pokémon can stand up to it?

Flaaffy™
(Electric)

Weezing™
(Poison)

Bayleef™
(Grass)

3. Plusle, an Electric Pokémon, charges onto the scene. Which of these Pokémon has the best chance of taking it down?

Phanpy™
(Ground)

Octillery™
(Water)

Taillow™
(Normal/Flying)

Check page 45 or your
Pokédex books for
the answers.

Which Pokémon Doesn't Belong?

Look at the three Pokémon in each row.
Two Pokémon are related by Evolution. Ca
you pick out which Pokémon is *not* related

1.

Sandshrew™   Nidorina™   Sandslash™

2.

Omastar™   Omanyte™   Shellder™

3.

Golem™   Graveler™   Machamp™

4. Kakuna™   Pupitar™   Larvitar™

5. Lileep™   Tropius™   Cradily™

6. Wobbuffet™   Quagsire™   Wooper™

7. Lairon™   Rhydon™   Aggron™

43

Check page 45, your *Rock & Ground Pokédex*, or your *Ultimate Sticker Book* for the answers.

Rock & Ground Pokémon Jokes

What kind of music does Geodude like best?

Rock and Roll!

What do you get when you cross a Groudon with a Diglett?

Huge holes all over your backyard!

How does Marowak call its friends?

On the tele-bone!

What does Phanpy have in common with a car?

They both have trunks!

How do you get a baby Onix to fall asleep?

You rock it!

What did the Nosepass say to the Pokémon Trainer?

Don't take me for granite.

44

Answers

Page 37: Who's That Rock Pokémon?

Sudowoodo!

Pages 38–39: A Rock/Ground Challenge

1. Cubone is Ground and Sudowoodo is Rock
2. Gligar is Ground/Flying and Aerodactyl is Rock/Flying
3. Lunatone is Rock/Psychic and Baltoy is Ground/Psychic
4. Steelix is Steel/Ground and Aron is Steel/Rock
5. Relicanth is Water/Rock and Wooper is Water/Ground
6. Nosepass is Rock and Donphan is Ground
7. Anorith is Rock/Bug and Diglett is Ground

Pages 40–41: Battle Time!

1. Makuhita (Fighting beats Rock)
2. Bayleef (Grass beats Ground)
3. Phanpy (Ground beats Electric)

Pages 42–43: Which Pokémon Doesn't Belong?

1. Nidorina
2. Shellder
3. Machamp
4. Kakuna
5. Tropius
6. Wobbuffet
7. Rhydon

45